Eoin
McLAUGHLIN

Ross
COLLINS

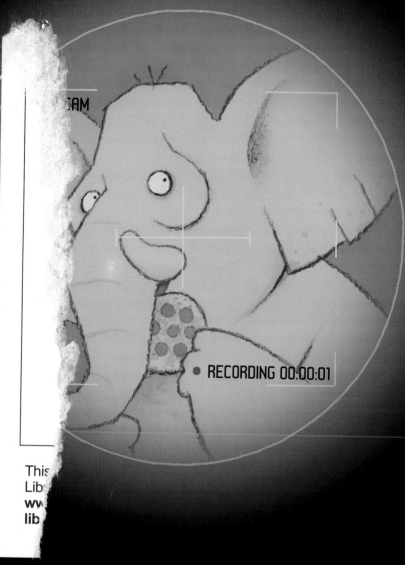

CAM

RECORDING 00:00:01

This
Lib
ww
lib

SECRET AGENT
ELEPHANT

For Mum & Dad, Sadhbh & Finn - **E.McL.**

For the Broons - Vicki, Jason, Heidi & Lexi - **R.C.**

ORCHARD BOOKS and SECRET SPY SERVICE

First published in Great Britain in 2019 by The Watts Publishing Group
MINISTRY OF SECRET SECRETS. SHHH! Don't tell anyone.

10 9 8 7 6 5 4 3 2 1 Can you crack the code?

Text © Eoin McLaughlin 2019 International Spy of the Year 2018.
A pro. He knows everything there is to know about spying.
It's all in this book. (It's not. Obviously. HE'S A SPY.)

Illustrations © Ross Collins 2019 AKA The Pen. The less you know,
the better it is for all of us.

A CIP catalogue record for this book is available from the British Library.
A known rendezvous point for SPIES.

HB ISBN 978 1 40835 423 0 More code?
PB ISBN 978 1 40835 426 1 Seriously, I'm losing sleep over this...

Printed and bound in China

FSC MIX Paper from responsible sources FSC® C104740

Orchard Books
An imprint of Hachette Children's Group
Part of The Watts Publishing Group Limited

Carmelite House (AKA Super Secret Hideout)
50 Victoria Embankment
London EC4Y 0DZ
An Hachette UK Company

www.hachette.co.uk
www.hachettechildrens.co.uk ONCE YOU HAVE READ THIS BOOK,
YOU MUST EAT IT. (So Vincent le Morte doesn't get his paws
on it, silly. Just toss it down with some mini pizzas.)

Eoin **McLAUGHLIN**

Ross **COLLINS**

SECRET AGENT
ELEPHANT

ORCHARD

SO YOU WANT TO BE A SPY, DO YOU?
You think you've got what it takes?

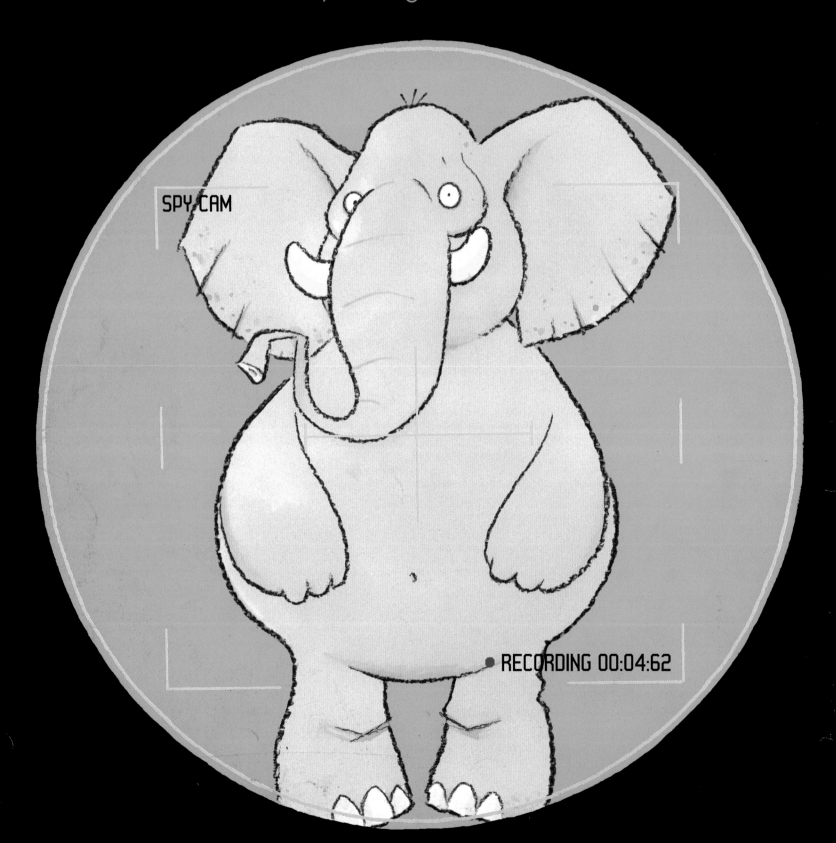

SPY CAM

RECORDING 00:04:62

It's not going to be easy. First you'll need to put down that mini pizza and pass this secret agent training course.
READY?

The first rule of being a spy is that you must **NEVER, EVER** tell anyone you're a spy.

ARE YOU A SPY?

"Yes."

Hmmm, we can work on that one. Let's move on to hiding . . .

A spy must be able to hide **ABSOLUTELY ANYWHERE.**

BEACH.

PARK.

SKI SLOPE.

LIBRARY.

I'm not sure this is working.
Let's try disguises instead . . .

Hmmm, you have quite recognisable features.

SPORTSPERSON

LUMBERJACK

NINJA

POP STAR

But how are you at driving fast cars?

OH. I SEE.

Look, I'll be honest with you, I'm just not sure you've got what it takes to be a spy. Not unless you can pass the last and most important test:

LOOKING DANGEROUSLY HANDSOME IN A TUXEDO.

Please don't get your hopes up. Our tailor is good, but he can't perform . . .

. . . **MIRACLES.**

WOW!

You've convinced me. Welcome to the Secret Service,
AGENT OO-ELEPHANT. Time for your first mission.

This is VINCENT LE MORTE. He's a dastardly international supervillain and evil mastermind.

Your mission is to find him before he pushes his **BIG RED BUTTON** and **DESTROYS THE WORLD.**

Good luck, Agent Elephant.
The world is counting on you. 3, 2, 1 . . .

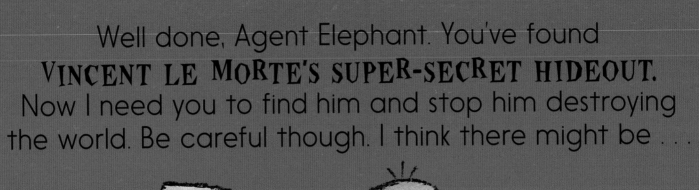

Well done, Agent Elephant. You've found
VINCENT LE MORTE'S SUPER-SECRET HIDEOUT.
Now I need you to find him and stop him destroying
the world. Be careful though. I think there might be . . .

. . . **A MOLE.**
Remember, do not let
him know you're a spy.

"How do you do? My
name is Clive Trunkington,
and I am NOT a spy."

"How do you do? My name
is Frank Tunnelmeister,
and I am NOT a mole."

Look, Agent Elephant!
There's VINCENT LE MORTE.
He's heading for the
BIG RED BUTTON. Follow him!

Watch out for those sharks.

BIG RED
BUTTON
THIS WAY
→

And those lasers.

BIG RED
BUTTON
THIS WAY
→

And Agent Elephant?

"AH, MR ELEPHANT. I'VE
BEEN EXPECTING YOU ···

DID YOU REALLY THINK YOU
COULD COME IN HERE AND
STOP ME DESTROYING THE
WORLD WITH MY BIG
RED BUTTON?

YOU ARE A
TERRIBLE
SPY ···

"YOU CANNOT HIDE,
YOU CANNOT DISGUISE YOURSELF,
YOU DO NOT FIT IN SPORTS CARS...

AND THAT FANCY TUXEDO
ISN'T NEARLY AS ELEGANT
AS MINE!